SECOND GRADE BABY

Look for these
and other books
in
The Kids in Ms. Colman's Class series

Jannie, Bobby, Tammy, Sara
Ian, Leslie, Hank, Terri
Nancy, Omar, Audrey, Chris, Ms. Colman
Karen, Hannie, Ricky, Natalie

The Kids in Ms. Colman's Class

Second Grade Baby

Ann M. Martin

Illustrations by Charles Tang

A
LITTLE
APPLE
PAPERBACK

SCHOLASTIC INC.

New York   Toronto   London   Auckland   Sydney
Mexico City   New Delhi   Hong Kong   Buenos Aires

No part of this publication may be reproduced in whole or in part, or stored in a retrieval system, or transmitted in any form or by any means, electronic, mechanical, photocopying, recording, or otherwise, without written permission of the publisher. For information regarding permission, write to Scholastic Inc., 555 Broadway, New York, NY 10012.

ISBN 0-590-69200-3

Copyright © 1996 by Ann M. Martin. All rights reserved. Published by Scholastic Inc. LITTLE APPLE PAPERBACKS and the LITTLE APPLE PAPERBACKS logo are trademarks of Scholastic Inc.

12 11 10 9   6 7 8 9/0

Printed in the U.S.A   40

First Scholastic printing, November 1996

*This book is for
Kate Gibbel*

NATALIE SPRINGER

Natalie Springer yawned and stretched. She sat up in bed. She peered out the window. It was still dark outside. As dark as midnight. But Natalie knew it was time to get up. She liked getting up early, when it was still dark. When she felt as if she were the only one in the world who was awake.

Let me see, Natalie thought. Today is Monday, the first day of the week. Goody. Five days of school before the weekend.

Natalie liked school very much. She especially liked Ms. Colman. Ms. Colman was her wonderful second-grade teacher at Stoneybrook Academy. Natalie was not so crazy about the weekend. That was because there was no school on the weekend. And when there was no school, Natalie sometimes felt lonely. She did not have many friends. And she did not have a single best friend. So on the weekends hardly anyone ever came to her house to play. But during the week, Natalie saw the other kids at school.

Natalie switched on her light. She opened her closet door. What did she feel like wearing to school that day? The other kids thought Natalie was a baby, so Natalie tried to find a grown-up-looking outfit. Her fuzzy kitten sweater? No. Her Barney and Baby Bop shirt? No way. Finally she settled on a plain red sweater and her blue jeans. Blue jeans were good because they would hide Natalie's socks, which were always falling down. Sometimes the kids at school teased Natalie about her drooping socks. Natalie did not know how the other kids managed to keep their own socks up. But she had decided not to spend much time worrying about it. Life was too short.

Natalie looked at the red sweater. She had not worn it in a long time. She hoped it still fit. She hoped —

"Hey!" Natalie cried. "What is *that*?" She was looking at something sewn inside the collar of her sweater. It was a small white tag. It read:

Natalie Springer
62 Elm Street
Stoneybrook, CT 06800

"Aughh!" Natalie shrieked. Where had *that* come from? What a horrible babyish tag. Natalie could not wear a sweater with a name tag in it. Name tags were for four-year-olds. Natalie was seven. She stuffed the sweater back on a shelf in the closet. She pulled out a striped sweater. She checked the collar. Another name tag! This was awful. Natalie looked in her kitten sweater. She looked in the Barney shirt.

3

She looked in her jeans. Name tag, name tag, name tag.

Mrs. Springer had gone on a sewing spree. Everywhere Natalie looked she found another name tag. They were sewn in her underwear and her socks, in her dresses and shirts. Natalie found one on her pillowcase and two more on her sheets. She even found one sewn inside the knitted cap on Buzzy Bear, her beloved teddy.

"Mommy!" cried Natalie.

"What is it?" Mrs. Springer hurried into Natalie's room. She was still wearing her nightgown. "Are you sick?"

"No! Mommy, why are these name tags everywhere?"

Mrs. Springer smiled. "Oh. In case you get your clothes mixed up at ballet class or during gym or at a sleepover. We will always know which ones are yours."

Natalie sighed. She knew her mother was trying to help her. But this was no help at all.

2

UNDERWEAR

Natalie stood alone in her room. Her bed was covered with clothes. In every single one was a name tag. Natalie thought about cutting the tags off, but they were sewn in quite tightly. Besides, her mother had worked very hard. The sewing had taken her a long time.

Natalie reached for the red sweater and the jeans. And underwear and socks. Only her sneakers had escaped name tags. She hoped the kids at school would not see the babyish tags, but she had a feeling they would be noticed one day. Probably very soon. And then the kids would chant, "Baby, baby, baby! Kindergarten baby!"

Well, that was not quite true, thought Natalie as she walked into her classroom that morning. Not all the kids would do that.

Natalie sat at her desk. She looked around. Natalie sat in the front row. That was because she wore glasses. Ms. Colman thought the glasses-wearers could see better in the front row. Ms. Colman knew about things like that. Ms. Colman wore glasses herself. (And anyway, Ms. Colman knew about lots of things.)

Natalie looked at Karen Brewer in the back row. Karen was one of the kids who probably would not tease Natalie. Karen was not a teaser. She talked too much, and she bragged and boasted and showed off. But she did not tease. (Usually.) Karen was lucky. She had *two* best friends, Hannie Papadakis and Nancy Dawes. Karen and Hannie and Nancy sat together in the last row. Hannie and Nancy probably would not tease Natalie, either.

Natalie watched as the other kids entered the classroom. There were Ricky Torres, Bobby Gianelli, and Hank Reubens. Definite teasers. There were Jannie Gilbert and Leslie Morris, best friends and more teasers. There were Tammy and Terri Barkans, the twins. They would not tease. They were Natalie's friends. There were Ian Johnson and Chris Lamar. Probably teasers, but it was hard to tell. There was Sara Ford. She was new that year, and would not tease. And there was Audrey Green, another definite teaser.

Natalie checked her clothes. Good. None of the tags showed. If she were very, *very*, VERY careful, perhaps she could keep them hidden.

When Ms. Colman entered the room, Natalie began to feel cheerful. First of all, Ms. Colman always made her feel cheerful. Second, Natalie realized she had been sitting in her classroom for almost twenty minutes and no one had seen a name tag. That was a good sign. A very good sign.

Ms. Colman picked up her book of lesson plans.

Knock knock.

Who was at the door? It was very early in the morning for a visitor.

Ms. Colman opened the door to Room 2A. "Well! Hello, Mrs. Springer," Natalie heard Ms. Colman say.

Mrs. Springer? What was Natalie's mother doing at school?

Ms. Colman and Mrs. Springer stepped into the room. "Hi, Ms. Colman," Mrs. Springer replied. "I just brought this for Natalie." Mrs. Springer held up a brown paper bag. "She forgot it this morning. It is her underwear. Her ballet lesson is this afternoon, and Natalie needs a change of clothes." Mrs. Springer waved to Natalie. Then she left.

Ms. Colman gave the bag to Natalie. She sat down at her desk and looked at her lesson plans. Then she poked her head into Mr. Berger's room next door. Mr. Berger was the other second-grade teacher. A door joined the two classrooms.

Bobby grabbed the paper bag.

"I want to see Natalie's underwear!" he cried.

"Me, too!" shouted Hank.

Before Natalie knew it, every kid in her class had seen her underwear. And every kid had seen the name tags.

I am dead meat, said Natalie to herself.

3

OMAR

The moment Ms. Colman returned to the classroom, the kids quieted down. Bobby tossed the underwear bag back to Natalie. Natalie stuffed it inside her desk. (She gave it a little pinch because she was mad at it.)

All around her, the kids were smirking. Bobby and Hank were turning red from trying not to laugh.

Ms. Colman took attendance. Natalie counted as Ms. Colman made checkmarks in her book. Check, check, check . . . fifteen checks in all. Hmm. Someone was missing. Someone was absent.

"Girls and boys," said Ms. Colman

11

then. "I have something to tell you. Omar is absent today. He is in the hospital."

"The *hos*pital?" exclaimed Karen Brewer.

"Yes," replied Ms. Colman. "Omar cut his hand and the cut became infected. He will be in the hospital for just two days. And he will be back in school on Thursday. But I thought we might make get well cards for him. I can take them to the hospital this afternoon."

Natalie looked around the classroom. The kids had stopped giggling. They were not even smiling. They were all thinking about Omar and the hospital. This was serious.

Later that morning, Ms. Colman handed out colored paper and markers. Natalie carefully made a beautiful card for Omar. So did the other kids. They still looked very serious. Maybe they had forgotten about Natalie's underwear and the name tags.

On Thursday, Omar returned to school, just as Ms. Colman had said he would. (That was one reason Natalie loved Ms. Colman. Ms. Colman always kept her promises.) Omar's hand was in a bandage. Otherwise, he seemed fine.

"Tell us about the hospital, Omar!" begged Natalie's classmates.

"Omar can do that during Show and Share," said Ms. Colman.

When it was time for Show and Share,

Ms. Colman called on Omar first.

"The hospital," Omar began, as he stood before the class, "was very boring. The food was not so great. But it was not bad, either. The doctors and nurses were nice. I had lots of visitors. And I got some nice presents. But mostly I was bored, bored, bored."

Hmmm. Bored, thought Natalie. Now isn't that interesting.

4

NATALIE'S GREAT IDEA

After Omar sat down, Ms. Colman took her place in the front of the classroom. "Now *I* have something to share with you," she said. "We are about to begin a new project. We will work on it together. As a class."

Natalie squirmed in her seat. She smiled to herself. This sounded exciting.

"It is a project," Ms. Colman continued, "that another teacher thought up. She tried it with her second-grade class. I read about it in a magazine.

"The project began," Ms. Colman went

on, "when the teacher brought a teddy bear to school. The bear's name was Rudy. The teacher made a tag for Rudy and fastened it to his shirt. This is what the tag said: *My name is Rudy. I am on an adventure. When you find me, please take me with you for several days. Then leave me in a public place for someone else to find. Send a postcard about your adventure with me to this address.* And the teacher had written out the address of her classroom. She left Rudy in an airport. Sure enough, someone found Rudy. It was a woman on vacation. She wrote to the class saying she had taken Rudy to Florida. Rudy had gone to the beach with her, and then ridden on Space Mountain at Disney World. Then she left Rudy in a restaurant in the Magic Kingdom. And another person found Rudy. That person took Rudy to New York City. Pretty soon, the kids in the class were receiving postcards and letters and even photos of Rudy from all around the world. Rudy had lots of adventures."

"Cool!" exclaimed Hannie Papadakis.

"Awesome," said Chris Lamar.

Audrey Green raised her hand. "Did Rudy come back to the class?" she asked.

Ms. Colman smiled. "Oh, yes. I forgot about that part. On the back of the tag, the teacher wrote: *If you find me after March fifteenth, please return me to the address on the front of this tag*. And sure enough, on April third, Rudy returned to school. Someone found him in Switzerland, and mailed him home."

"Excellent," said Ricky, nodding his head.

"And so," continued Ms. Colman, "we are going to send a teddy bear on an adventure, too. We can follow its trip on a map, and learn about the places it visits."

"Does it have to be a teddy bear?" asked Jannie Gilbert.

"No," replied Ms. Colman. "It could be a doll or another kind of stuffed animal."

"Where will we get the doll or stuffed animal?" asked Nancy Dawes.

"Anyone who wants to," said Ms. Colman, "may bring in an animal or doll tomorrow. We will vote on which one will take the trip. And we will ask that it be sent back to us by December first."

Natalie was trying to pay attention to Ms. Colman. But her mind was wandering. Just a little bit. It had wandered back to what Omar had said about the hospital. That the hospital was boring, boring, boring.

Natalie raised her hand. "Ms. Colman?" she said. "I have an idea."

"Yes, Natalie?"

"I was thinking that when our project is over, we could put all the postcards and things in an album. Then we could take the album to the hospital. We could leave it there so the kids who are stuck in the hospital could read about the exciting adventure. Then they would not be so bored."

"Hey! That is a great idea!" cried Karen.

"Indoor voice, Karen," Ms. Colman reminded her.

"It *is* a great idea," said Sara quietly.

Natalie looked around her. The other kids agreed. Natalie's idea was great.

"That is just what the kids in the hospital need," said Omar.

"We can make the album really special," said Leslie Morris.

Everyone began talking at once.

No one mentioned underwear. Or name tags.

Natalie smiled. Then she grinned.

She grinned at Ms. Colman, and Ms. Colman grinned back at her.

5

BUZZY BEAR

Natalie swallowed the last of her apple juice. She ate the last bite of her Oreo cookie. Then she carried the tin can her juice had come in to a bin at the back of the cafeteria. It was a recycling bin, and Natalie was careful to recycle. It was important to her.

"Want to play hopscotch?" Terri Barkan asked when Natalie returned to the table. "Tammy and I are going to play."

"Sure," replied Natalie. The kids had been pretty nice to her all morning. Natalie thought it was because of her good idea about giving the special project to the kids in the hospital.

On the playground, Terri and Tammy
and Natalie found smooth stones for their
hopscotch game. The twins let Natalie go
first. As Natalie hopped along, Terri said to
Tammy, "We could bring in Tootsie tomorrow."

"Tootsie? Who's Tootsie?" asked Natalie.

"Our stuffed elephant," replied Terri.
"Maybe Tootsie could go on the adventure."

"Wait, you bring Tootsie, and I will

bring Taffy," said Tammy. "Taffy is our stuffed chipmunk," she told Natalie.

Sara Ford wandered by. She had stopped to watch the game. While Tammy took her turn, Sara said, "I am going to bring in my Barbie tomorrow."

"Your *Barbie*?" repeated Terri. "That is very brave. She might not come back, you know. Ms. Colman said so."

"I know," replied Sara. "I will take that chance."

"Wow . . ." said Natalie slowly. That

was brave of Sara. Ms. Colman had indeed said there was a chance the teddy or doll that was sent on the trip might not be returned. It might get lost somewhere, or someone might decide to keep it (even though that would be stealing, Natalie noted). Or someone might decide that mailing a teddy back to Stoneybrook, Connecticut, was just too much trouble.

"*I* am going to bring in Goosie tomorrow," said Karen Brewer. She was watching the game with Hannie and Nancy.

"You *are*? Your stuffed cat?" cried Hannie. "But you love Goosie."

"Well, I am brave, too," said Karen.

"And — and so am I," said Jannie Gilbert. "I am going to bring in Sleepytime Susie. My best doll."

"I wonder if the boys will be brave enough to bring in anything," said Karen. She glanced at Bobby and Omar playing soccer nearby.

"I heard that," said Omar. "And I am going to bring in my old giraffe."

24

"What are you going to bring, Natalie?" asked Nancy Dawes.

"I — I am going to bring . . . well, I have so many choices. I have not decided yet. I will decide tonight."

That night, Natalie sat on her bed. Spread out around her were her dolls and Buzzy Bear. Buzzy Bear was Natalie's only stuffed animal. She liked dolls better than animals. Except for Buzzy Bear. Buzzy was Natalie's favorite toy in the world. He had been given to her by her grandfather on the day she was born. Natalie had never, ever spent a night without Buzzy. He came with her on vacations. He came with her on sleepovers. Could Natalie really part with Buzzy for two or three months? What if Buzzy never came back?

Natalie thought and thought. She wanted to be brave like the other kids. She wanted to show them she was not a baby, even if her mother *had* sewn name tags everywhere. Natalie looked at her dolls. She could bring in one of them. Maybe. Well, no. Her dolls were all pretty ratty, and most of them were naked. The boys would tease her forever if she brought in one of her dolls.

That left Buzzy Bear.

Natalie sighed. She laid Buzzy on her pillow.

"Okay," she said to him. "Tomorrow you are going to have a special treat. Tomorrow I am going to take you to school with me."

6
TO WHOM IT MAY CONCERN

The next day, Buzzy Bear rode to school in Natalie's lap. Natalie was feeling a lot better than she had felt the night before. This was because she had thought of something wonderful. Natalie had realized that just because she brought Buzzy to school did not mean that Buzzy would go on the trip. Someone else's teddy would probably be chosen, and that would be just fine. Natalie could bring Buzzy to her room, and the kids would see how brave she was. But then they would choose a different animal, and Natalie could take

Buzzy home with her at the end of the day. Perfect.

So now Natalie hopped out of the car. " 'Bye, Daddy!" she called to her father. And she ran into school with Buzzy. She was not worried one little bit. "I hope you like school, Buzzy," she whispered.

Natalie sat at her desk. She put Buzzy in her lap. She watched the other kids arrive. Natalie decided she would try to guess which doll or animal would be chosen to make the trip. (She had a feeling it might be Sleepytime Susie.)

Okay. There was Jannie. But where was Sleepytime Susie? Hmm. Jannie must have forgotten her.

And now there was Sara. But where was her Barbie?

Natalie saw Terri and Tammy, but no Tootsie or Taffy. She saw Karen, but no Goosie. And she saw Omar, but no old giraffe.

Soon all of Natalie's classmates had arrived. And their desks were empty except for Buzzy Bear. Natalie could not stand it. She turned around and whispered to Tammy, "Where is Taffy?"

"I, um, decided not to bring her," replied Tammy.

"You mean, you chickened out," said Hank.

"Well, you were going to bring in your firefighter doll," said Tammy. "And I do not see that anywhere."

"I forgot it!" cried Hank.

"Liar," said Ian. "You chickened out, too. So did Omar."

"So did everyone," muttered Natalie.

Natalie looked at Buzzy. He was sitting on her desk wearing his knitted hat and coat. Natalie thought about stuffing him inside the desk, but he was too big for that. Besides, all the kids had seen him.

Later that morning, Ms. Colman stood before her class. "Where are your dolls and stuffed animals?" she asked.

The kids pointed silently to Buzzy Bear.

"That's it?" said Ms. Colman. "No one brought in anything else?"

The kids shook their heads.

"Well, then. Hmm." Ms. Colman smiled at Natalie. "I guess we do not even need to take a vote. Buzzy Bear it is. I hope you are ready for a big adventure, Buzzy."

Natalie tried to smile back at Ms. Colman.

Just then, Bobby Gianelli, of all people, tapped Natalie's arm. "You are really brave," he said to her.

"*Really* brave," added Audrey from behind her.

Natalie gulped. She nodded. She could not back out. Not now when the kids finally thought she was grown-up, and even brave.

Ms. Colman picked Buzzy up. "Well, let's see," she said. "I like your blue and yellow coat very much. It is the perfect thing to pin your traveling note to. Class, we are going to write Buzzy's note together. I will write it on the blackboard for now. When it is finished, we can copy it onto a tag for Buzzy. Okay. How should we begin our letter?"

Omar waved his hand in the air. "I know! It should start: To whom it may concern."

On the blackboard, Ms. Colman printed:

To Whom It May Concern:

GOOD-BYE, BUZZY BEAR

To Whom It May Concern:

Hello! My name is Buzzy Bear. I belong to Class 2A at Stoneybrook Academy in Stoneybrook, Connecticut. I would like to have some adventures. The kids in 2A would like to learn about other cities and countries. Please take me with you for a day or two. Then send a postcard or a letter or a photo to the address on the back of this tag so the kids in 2A will know what I have been up to. When our adventure is over, leave me in a place where someone else can find me. Eventually, Class 2A would like to have me back so I can go home with

33

Natalie Springer, who is my owner. Please return me by December 1st. Thank you!

That was the message Ms. Colman had written on a big cardboard tag. On the back of the tag, she had printed the address of Stoneybrook Academy. Then she had fastened the tag to Buzzy Bear's coat with a large safety pin.

"There," said Ms. Colman when she had finished.

Now Buzzy Bear was sitting on the edge of her desk. It was a very important day. Today Buzzy would leave on his adventure. When the kids in Ms. Colman's class entered their room that morning, Buzzy was the first thing they saw.

"Hi, Buzzy Bear," said Natalie as she sat at her desk. "Are you ready to go on your trip? You will be leaving soon."

"Are *you* ready to let Buzzy go on his trip?" Ms. Colman asked Natalie.

Natalie nodded. "Yup." She was not

going to let her classmates down.

Shortly before lunchtime, Natalie heard a knock at the door. She looked up from her reading book. Ms. Colman was opening the door.

"Hello, Susan," she said.

"Hello." A smiling woman entered the room. She was carrying a briefcase. She looked at Ms. Colman's desk. "Is that Buzzy Bear?"

"It certainly is," replied Ms. Colman. Ms. Colman faced her class. "Girls and boys," she said, "this is my friend Susan Ying. She is going on a business trip today. She has agreed to take Buzzy Bear with her to the airport. She will leave him for the first person to find."

"Are you ready for your trip, Buzzy?" asked Susan Ying.

Buzzy just sat on Ms. Colman's desk. The tag was so big that it hid part of his face. Natalie could see only one of his eyes.

Natalie raised her hand. "Um, Ms.

Ying?" she said. "I am Natalie Springer. Buzzy is my bear. And I think he is ready for the trip. Do you know where you will leave him when you get to the airport?"

"I think I will leave him in a waiting area — at a gate where a lot of people are waiting for a flight. Either that or I will leave him in a restaurant at the airport."

Natalie nodded. "Okay."

Ms. Colman handed Buzzy to Susan Ying. "Thank you so much for doing this," she said. "We really appreciate it."

"I am happy to do it," replied Ms. Ying. "I will call you later."

"Good-bye! Good-bye, Buzzy!" called the kids as Ms. Ying carried him out the door. "Have a good trip!"

"Good-bye, Buzzy!" Natalie called along with her friends. Then she whispered, "I love you."

Just before the bell rang at the end of the day, the office secretary came to the door of 2A. He handed a slip of paper to Ms. Colman. Ms. Colman read it. Then she turned to her students. "Class," she said, "this message is from Susan Ying. She called to say that she left Buzzy in a crowd of people waiting for a plane to Chicago."

Chicago, thought Natalie. That sounded awfully far away.

HELLO FROM CHICAGO

When the kids in Ms. Colman's class entered their room the next day, they saw something new. Ms. Colman had taken down the leaf pictures that had been tacked to the bulletin board. In their place was an enormous map. It was a map of every country in the world.

"That," said Ms. Colman, "is to help us keep track of Buzzy's trip. Each time we get a postcard from Buzzy, we will see where the card is from. We will circle that place on the map. And we will draw a line from there to the next place Buzzy visits. While we wait to hear from Buzzy, we can learn about the places he visits."

Natalie felt very impatient that morning. She had trouble sitting still. She wiggled and squirmed.

Finally she raised her hand. "Ms. Colman? When does the mail come to our school?"

"You mean what time of day? Lunchtime, I think," said Ms. Colman.

After recess that day, Natalie hurried

to her seat. "Ms. Colman, Ms. Colman! Is the mail here yet? Did we get a postcard from Buzzy?"

"Oh, Natalie. It is too soon to hear from Buzzy," said Ms. Colman. "I am sorry. I do not think we will hear from him for several more days."

"Several more *days*? Boo." Natalie slumped in her seat. How could she wait for several more days?

She did wait, of course. And on Tuesday afternoon when the kids in Ms. Colman's class returned to their seats after recess, their teacher was smiling. "I have great news," she said. She was holding a postcard.

"You heard from Buzzy!" shrieked Natalie. "What does the card say?"

Ms. Colman held it up so her students could see the picture. "It is a photo of the city of Chicago," said Ms. Colman. "And this is what Buzzy wrote: 'Dear Class Two-A, hello from the great city of Chicago! Right now I am traveling with Mr. Frank Saunders. He found me at the airport and took me on a plane with him. So far I have been to the Sears Tower, eaten lunch at the Hard Rock Cafe, and gone to a very boring business meeting. Yours truly, Buzzy.'"

Natalie heaved a deep sigh. Buzzy was safe. And he was having fun (except for the boring meeting). She raised her hand. "What is the Sears Tower?" she asked. "I am ready to learn about Chicago!"

BUZZY IN LONDON

During the next few days, the kids in Ms. Colman's class were very busy. Ms. Colman helped them find Chicago, Illinois, on the big map. Omar circled it with a red marker.

"I wonder where Buzzy will go next," said Audrey.

While they waited to find out, they learned about Chicago and about Illinois. They learned that the state bird of Illinois is the cardinal, and the state flower is the violet.

"Let's find out the bird and the flower for every state," said Karen. So they started a list.

They learned that Chicago is the largest city in Illinois, but that it is not the capital. The capital is Springfield. They learned that Illinois is sometimes called the Prairie State. Then they looked up some information about the Sears Tower. They found out that it is a skyscraper 110 stories high.

On Friday, another postcard arrived. This one said:

Dear Class 2A,

Hi, it is me, your friend Buzzy Bear! I am in Dallas, Texas, now. A girl found me in the airport in Chicago. (She is writing this for me.) Her name is Nora, and she is eleven. Nora took me to a Dallas Cowboys football game with her dad. The Cowboys won! It was exciting!!

Love,
Buzzy

Four days later, a letter arrived. It was from Wyoming. A man and a woman and their new baby had found Buzzy in a restaurant in Dallas. They took Buzzy with them on their vacation.

Chris Lamar had opened the letter. He was reading it to the class. "Hey! Here is a photo of Buzzy! He is riding a horse near . . . near . . . Grand Teton National Park." Chris held up the photo of Buzzy on horseback.

The kids in Ms. Colman's class circled two more cities on the map. They learned about Texas and Wyoming.

One day a card arrived with a different looking stamp.

"The card is from Canada!" exclaimed Bobby. "Buzzy is in another country. He is a foreign traveler."

A woman named Gina Seldon had found Buzzy in a department store. She had flown him to Calgary, Alberta.

"Brrrr! It is *cold* here," Buzzy wrote.

After the card from Alberta arrived, the kids did not hear from Buzzy for one whole long week. Finally, one Wednesday afternoon, Ms. Colman was holding up a

WYOMING
GRAND TETON
NATIONAL PARK

CHICAGO, IL.

DALLAS
TX

letter when her class returned from recess. She was smiling again. In fact, she was grinning. "You will never guess where this letter is from," she said.

"Is it from Alaska?" suggested Jannie.

"No. That is a good guess, though," said Ms. Colman. "Hank, why don't you read the letter to us."

Hank walked to the front of the room. He unfolded the thin sheet of blue paper. " 'Dear Class Two-A,' " he read. " 'Cheerio! It is me, Buzzy Bear. I am in London, England. Emily and Kathryn Shulman and their mom have taken me to the Tower of London and two museums . . .' "

The letter went on and on.

London, England, thought Natalie. What an adventure Buzzy is having. He is so lucky.

Buzzy's next card was from Paris, France. The next was from Milan, Italy, and the next was from Warsaw in Poland.

"He is a world traveler," Natalie announced proudly to her classmates. And they agreed, wide-eyed. "I wonder where he will go next," added Natalie.

She waited to hear. Her classmates waited to hear. Ms. Colman waited to hear. But two entire weeks crawled by with no word at all.

10
WHERE IS BUZZY?

At the end of two weeks, Natalie was worried. Buzzy was so far away. He had taken such a long trip. Until now, this had seemed wonderful. The classroom map was full of red circles. It was crisscrossed with red lines. The list of state birds and flowers was growing. And the kids had decided to make another list: state nicknames. Their state, Connecticut, was known as the Nutmeg State, which they thought was funny.

But now Natalie could not help worrying about Buzzy. Two weeks was a very long time. Where could he be? What could have happened?

"Well," said Ms. Colman, "remember that Buzzy is in Europe now. Lots and lots of different languages are spoken there. Maybe Buzzy has been found by someone who does not speak English. He would not be able to read Buzzy's tag. And he could not write a card or a letter for Buzzy."

Natalie tried to feel hopeful. But it was hard. Even Ms. Colman did not look very hopeful. She frowned each time the mail came, and there was no word from Buzzy.

After two more weeks went by, Natalie began to feel frightened. Now Buzzy had not been heard from in a month. She had known all along that it was possible — just possible — that Buzzy might be left somewhere and not found. Or that someone might find him who would not care about the class project. Someone could give Buzzy away, or put him somewhere and forget about him.

But *maybe*, Natalie said to herself, Ms. Colman is right. Someone, or several someones, have found Buzzy, but cannot read his tag. I will just have to keep waiting and hoping.

One evening, Natalie sat at the dinner table with her parents. She was trying to eat, but she was not very hungry.

"Is anything wrong?" asked Mr. Springer.

"We have not heard from Buzzy in a month," replied Natalie.

"That is a long time," said her mother.

"Yes." Natalie swallowed hard.

"We know you miss him," said her father.

"Yes," said Natalie again.

"And maybe you will hear from him soon," added Mrs. Springer. "A letter could come any day. Perhaps tomorrow."

Natalie nodded. Her parents wanted her to feel better. But when Natalie went to bed that night, she began to cry. She lay on her back and let her tears run down the sides of her face and into her ears.

She sniffled loudly. "Where are you, Buzzy Bear?" she asked. "I miss you." Natalie pulled aside her curtain. She stared outside at the full round moon. "Do you know, man-in-the-moon?"

The man-in-the-moon did not answer. After a long time, Natalie fell asleep.

That night, she did not sleep very well. She dreamed about Buzzy Bear. She dreamed that he was lost in a grocery store. He ran up and down the aisles, looking for Natalie. He tried to ask for help, but it turned out to be a French grocery store, and Buzzy did not speak French.

The next day, Natalie felt grumpy. She ate her breakfast silently. She rode to school with her father silently.

"Good-bye, Natalie! Have a good day at school!" called Mr. Springer.

" 'Bye," was all Natalie replied.

That morning, Ms. Colman collected homework and took attendance. Then she stood in front of her class. She looked very serious.

Uh-oh, thought Natalie.

"Boys and girls, I would like to talk to you about something," Ms. Colman began. "It is about Buzzy. We have not heard about him in over a month now, which is a long time. I am afraid I must tell you that I think there is a good chance Buzzy will not be coming back."

A Surprise For Natalie

Natalie stared at Ms. Colman.

"I am sorry, Natalie," said her teacher.

Natalie nodded. Her stomach hurt, as if someone had just kicked it. Natalie thought, I knew all along that Buzzy might not come back. But . . . I never believed it would happen.

Now that Natalie had heard Ms. Colman say so, though, it suddenly seemed very, very real.

"Natalie?" asked Ms. Colman.

Natalie could not speak. Before she knew what was happening, she began to

cry. Tears slid down her cheeks. She wiped them away, but she could not stop crying. All the other kids were looking at her.

And then Bobby began to snicker. So did Leslie. So did Jannie and Ian and Audrey. Hee, hee, hee. Their hands covered their mouths, but Natalie could hear them anyway. She could hear them just fine.

Natalie wiped away a few more tears in time to stare at the laughers. She gave them a Very Stern Look. With a Very Big Frown. She looked quite cross.

The gigglers stopped giggling.

"All right," said Ms. Colman. "That is enough. Quiet down, please. It is time for our science work, anyway. But first, let me see. I believe Mr. Posner left some papers in the office for me. Natalie, would you please go get them?"

Natalie stood up. She stalked out of the room.

As soon as she was gone, Ms. Colman said to her class, "Can you tell me why you laughed at Natalie just now?" She looked at Bobby, Jannie, Leslie, Ian, and Audrey.

No one said a word.

"I am serious," Ms. Colman went on. "I would really like to know why you laughed at her."

Bobby, Jannie, Leslie, Ian, and Audrey were staring down at their desks. Finally, Ian looked up. He raised his hand. "Um, because she was crying," he mumbled.

"And you thought that was funny?" Ms. Colman said.

"Well, it is just that sometimes Natalie is such a baby."

"Why do you think she was crying?" asked Ms. Colman. "Jannie?"

"Because she feels sad."

In the back of the room, Karen Brewer was wiggling around in her seat. She was waving her hand. "Ms. Colman! Ms. Colman!"

"Yes, Karen?"

"Ms. Colman, Natalie was crying because she feels bad that Buzzy Bear is not coming back. Buzzy is Natalie's only bear.

She loves him very much. But still, she brought him to school and she let him go on the trip. That was very brave of her." Karen paused. "Nobody *else* let any of *their* stuffed animals go," she said sternly.

"Thank you, Karen," said Ms. Colman.

Bobby raised his hand. "Maybe," he said slowly, "maybe we should do something nice for Natalie. Something to make her feel better."

"That would be a lot better than laughing at her," said Karen huffily.

"Okay, Karen. That is enough," said Ms. Colman.

Audrey brightened then. "I know! We could get another bear for Natalie. We could even get her another Buzzy Bear, exactly like the one she lost. I have seen them in Bellair's, the department store."

"Now *that* is a great idea," said Ms. Colman.

"We could all chip in some money," added Sara.

"And we could *surprise* Natalie with her new Buzzy," said Nancy.

"Fantastic," agreed Ms. Colman. "And now, class, Natalie will be back at any moment. So please open your books. And zip up your lips."

12

BUZZY TWO

Natalie hurried along the hallway. She was carrying an envelope for Ms. Colman. It was from Mr. Posner. It looked important. And Natalie felt important to have been trusted with it. She opened the door to 2A. Her classmates were reading their science books. They seemed very, very interested in them. Natalie handed the envelope to her teacher.

"Thank you, Natalie," said Ms. Colman.

"You're welcome."

Natalie returned to her seat. She was glad that no one said anything else to her. She was especially glad that no one giggled.

That afternoon, Natalie realized something very interesting. It was about Buzzy Bear. Natalie realized that she was doing all right without him. She still loved Buzzy, of course. And she missed him, and was very sad that he was gone. But she was doing all right. After all, Buzzy had now been away for quite awhile. And Natalie was pretty much the same. Or better. She had brought home an extra good report card. She had played at Karen's house a couple of times. She had even lost two teeth and grown half an inch. Her mother thought her feet were growing again, too, and that soon Natalie would need new sneakers.

All this without Buzzy, thought Natalie. Huh.

On Monday morning, Natalie hurried into her classroom. The bell was about to ring. The rest of the kids were already sitting at their desks. They grinned at Natalie as she ran to her seat.

Uh-oh, thought Natalie. I wonder what is wrong. She checked her clothes. No name tags were sticking out. Her underwear was not showing. She pulled up her socks. No one said anything. But no one stopped smiling, either.

After the morning announcements, Ms. Colman said, "Jannie? Karen? Would you come to the front of the room, please?"

Grinning more widely than ever, Jannie and Karen flew to the front of the room. They pulled a box out from under Ms. Colman's desk. Together they picked it up and set it on Natalie's desk.

"Natalie, this is for you from all of us," said Jannie.

"To say thank you for letting Buzzy go on the trip," added Karen.

"Oh — " Natalie started to say.

But Karen hurried on. "It was really, really nice of you to lend us Buzzy," she said. "No one else was brave enough to let their bears go away. We really, really appreciate what you did. And we — "

"And we want to say thank you," said Ms. Colman quickly.

"You're welcome," said Natalie.

"Open your present!" cried Karen.

Natalie looked at the big box. She untied the ribbon. She tore off the wrapping paper. Then she lifted the lid of the box, and pulled away some tissue paper. Staring up at her were the black button eyes of Buzzy Bear. Not her own Buzzy, Natalie realized. But another bear that looked very much like Buzzy. He was even wearing Buzzy's knitted hat and his blue and yellow coat.

"Wow," said Natalie. "Um, thanks. Thanks a lot."

"Guess what his name is," said Karen. "It is Buzzy Two."

"Buzzy Two," repeated Natalie. "Well . . . well, thanks."

When Natalie returned home from school that day, she took Buzzy Two to her room. She sat him on her bed in Buzzy's old spot. But he did not look quite right there. So Natalie moved him to her bookshelf. She put him with some other toys.

Natalie knew a secret. Her secret was that she liked Buzzy Two. But she did not need him.

LOVE, MARY

Another week went by without word from Buzzy. It was almost winter now. The days were short and cold.

One afternoon when Natalie's mother picked her up after school, she said, "Honey, a package came for you today."

"What?" said Natalie. She had not been listening. She had been looking out the car window at the dark sky. She was wondering if it might snow soon. "I got a package?" she said.

"Yes. All the way from Ireland. Isn't that odd? We do not know anyone in Ireland."

"Ireland," repeated Natalie. "I know

where that is." She thought of the map on the wall in her classroom. "It is near Scotland. The capital is Dublin. Who is the package from?"

"Someone named Mary Bowen."

Hmm. Mary Bowen. Natalie wondered about Mary and the package all the way home. As soon as her mother parked the car, Natalie hopped out. She ran inside. The package was sitting on a bench in the hallway.

"Here, honey. Let me help you," said Mrs. Springer. She found a pair of scissors and cut the tape that was wound around the box.

Natalie looked at the address. Just as her mother had said, the box had been mailed by Mary Bowen from Dublin, Ireland.

"Her handwriting looks just like mine, Mommy," said Natalie. "I bet Mary Bowen is seven, too."

"But who on earth could she be?" asked Mrs. Springer.

When the tape had been cut away, Natalie opened the top of the carton. The first thing she saw was an envelope with her name on it. Natalie opened the envelope. She pulled out a letter. It said:

Dear Natalie,

You do not know me. My name is Mary Bowen. I am eight years old. I live in Dublin, Ireland. That is very far away from you. I suppose you are wondering how I got your name and address. Well, that is a good story. I found them inside the hat of this bear.

"This bear!" cried Natalie. "This *bear*?!"

Natalie let Mary's letter fall to the floor. She shoved aside the newspaper in the box. And she pulled out . . . Buzzy Bear.

"The *real* Buzzy!" Natalie cried. "Oh, he is *back*! Mary found Buzzy and she sent him *back*! But why didn't she send him to school? That was what the note on his tag said to do. And *where* did she find my ad-

FROM: MARY BOWEN,
DUBLIN,
IRELAND.

dress? Oh, my gosh. I cannot believe Buzzy is back!"

Mrs. Springer was smiling. "Buzzy's tag must have come off," she said. "See, Natalie? He looks a little bedraggled. Now let's see how Mary found your home address." Mrs. Springer took off Buzzy's cap.

"Oh! Oh, it is the name tag!" exclaimed Natalie. "You sewed one of my name tags in Buzzy's hat! Boy, I thought that was silly when you did it. But now I am glad!"

Natalie read the rest of Mary's letter. It told how Mary had found Buzzy while she was waiting in the Dublin airport. He was stuck behind a seat. Mary had started to play with Buzzy when she saw the name tag with Natalie's address on it. The end of her letter said:

I knew you would want your teddy back. If he were mine and I lost him, I would want him back. So I am sending him to you now. My mum is helping me. (She is the person my dad and I were waiting to meet at the airport.) Have fun with your bear.

Love,

Mary

"Oh, this is too wonderful!" said Natalie.

"This was awfully nice of Mary," added Mrs. Springer.

"I want to write to her and thank her. Can I?" asked Natalie.

"Of course."

So Natalie settled down at the kitchen table. A piece of her mother's best writing paper was in front of her. In her lap sat Buzzy.

Dear Mary, Natalie began.

NATALIE'S GIFT

That night, Natalie slept with Buzzy Bear again. It was just like old times. Except that when Natalie woke the next morning, she found Buzzy on the floor. "You must have fallen out of bed during the night," she said. "And I did not even notice."

When Natalie left for school later, Buzzy was tucked under her arm. In her school bag was the letter from Mary.

"Hey, you brought Buzzy Two to school!" exclaimed Jannie, when Natalie entered the classroom. "That's nice."

Natalie just smiled. She did not say anything.

Not until Show and Share.

But during Show and Share time, Natalie brought her bear to the front of the class. Then she read Mary's letter aloud.

"You mean that is the *real* Buzzy Bear?" cried Jannie.

"Oh, Natalie. How wonderful," said Ms. Colman.

The kids gathered around Buzzy. They examined him. They looked at the name tag in his hat. (They did not laugh.)

"Well," said Ms. Colman, "I guess we will never know exactly what happened to Buzzy. We will never know how he got from Poland to Ireland, how he lost his tag, or how he got stuffed down behind a seat in the airport. But at least he is back."

"So we have an end to our story," said Chris.

"We could finish the book about his adventures," added Natalie.

"And take it to the hospital," said Omar.

The kids set to work. They got out all

of the postcards, letters, and photos from Buzzy. They lined them up in the order they had received them. Then they found a small map of the world, one that would fit in an album. They traced Buzzy's journey on it. They copied their lists of state birds and flowers and nicknames.

Ms. Colman let Natalie make the cover for the book about Buzzy. Natalie wrote THE ADVENTURES OF BUZZY BEAR in very beautiful letters. Under it, she glued a picture of Buzzy.

Then the kids began the job of gluing everything into the album. The first thing they glued down was the story of their project. Then they glued down the things Buzzy had sent from his trip. They wrote a caption under each one to explain what it was.

When Mary's letter had been glued down on the last page, Ms. Colman said, "I think our project is ready."

Natalie raised her hand. "Almost ready," she said. "I have one more thing to go with the album." Natalie stood up. She walked to Ms. Colman's desk. She set Buzzy Bear on the album.

"Oh, that is lovely, Natalie," said Ms. Colman. "You are going to let the kids at the hospital see Buzzy in person."

"No," said Natalie. "I am going to *give* them Buzzy. I do not need him anymore. But I bet the kids in the hospital do."

"Why don't you give them Buzzy Two?" asked Nancy.

Natalie shook her head. "You gave me Buzzy Two. He was a present from all of you. That was very special. So I do not want to give him away. But the kids in the hospital should have the real Buzzy to go with the album."

Ms. Colman was smiling at Natalie. Natalie smiled back. Then she grinned at her classmates.

"Hey, I have an idea," said Audrey. "Ms. Colman, could Mr. Berger take a picture of us with Buzzy and the album? We could hang it on our bulletin board. Then we will always remember Buzzy and his trip and our project."

So Mr. Berger came into the room with his Polaroid camera.

"Say cheese!" he said.

15

THE ADVENTURES OF BUZZY BEAR

"Is it time to line up?"

"Wait, I cannot find my boots."

"Is Buzzy Bear ready? Where is the album?"

"Karen, you are my partner today."

Natalie looked around the classroom. Everyone was very excited. In just a few minutes they would climb on a yellow school bus and ride to the hospital. It was time to visit the kids there, and give them Buzzy and the album.

"Okay, class. Line up at the door," said Ms. Colman.

The kids found their bus partners. They lined up with them by the door. Then they followed Ms. Colman down the hall, out the front door, and into the parking lot. Natalie's mother and the twins' father followed behind *them*. (They were the room parents for the trip.)

"All aboard!" called the bus driver.

Natalie and Hannie were the first two on the bus. Natalie carried Buzzy, and Hannie carried the album.

"Everybody! Everybody! I have to tell you something!" called Omar. He was waving his hand back and forth.

"Yes, what is it?" asked Ms. Colman as the bus turned onto the street.

"I have to tell everyone about the hospital," said Omar. "Since I was in it not long ago, I know all about it. Now," he went on, "kids usually are *not* allowed to visit people in the hospital, not even other kids. So we will not be able to see the playroom in the kids' wing. The playroom is where the nurses will probably put Buzzy and the album after we leave today. And it is very boring. There are just a few broken-down old toys in it, but Buzzy will cheer it up."

"Omar is right," said Ms. Colman. "We cannot go upstairs when we get to the hospital. We are going to go to a special room downstairs. The doctors and nurses are going to bring some kids there to meet us. They are kids who do not have to worry about catching germs from us."

"They probably have broken legs and stuff," said Omar importantly. "They will be really glad to see us."

Natalie glanced at Hannie. "Are you nervous?" she asked.

"A little," said Hannie.

"Me, too," said Natalie. She clutched Buzzy Bear tightly.

A few minutes later, the bus pulled up in front of the hospital.

"Last stop!" called the driver.

Ms. Colman led the kids inside.

A doctor met them at the door. "You

must be the kids in Ms. Colman's class," she said. "My name is Dr. Longwood. Thank you so much for coming. The children are waiting for you."

Dr. Longwood took the kids to a big room. It was decorated with streamers and balloons. Natalie saw that eight kids were waiting for them. Many of them were in wheelchairs. Two kids were on crutches. One girl was bald.

At first, Natalie and her friends did not know what to say or do. So Ms. Colman told the story of Buzzy and his adventures. Then she explained that her students were going to give the kids the album. "Along with something else," she added. "Natalie?"

"Along with the real Buzzy," said Natalie, and she held him up.

"Cool," said the girl who was bald.

"Is he really for us?" asked a boy in a wheelchair.

"He really is," replied Natalie. She handed Buzzy to the boy.

The kids crowded around. They patted Buzzy. They looked at the name tag. They turned the pages in the album.

"Buzzy is famous!" exclaimed one girl.

"Thank you for Buzzy," another girl said to Natalie.

"You're welcome," replied Natalie.

The kids in Ms. Colman's class visited for a while. When it was time to go, they called good-bye to Dr. Longwood and the kids. Then they turned to leave. And Natalie whispered, "Good-bye, Buzzy. I still love you."

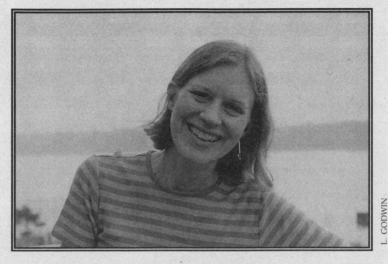

L. GODWIN

About the Author

ANN M. MARTIN lives in New York City and loves animals, especially cats. She has two cats of her own, Gussie and Woody.

Other books by Ann M. Martin that you might enjoy are *Stage Fright*; *Me and Katie (the Pest)*; and the books in *The Baby-sitters Club* series.

Ann likes ice cream and *I Love Lucy*. And she has her own little sister, whose name is Jane.

THE KIDS IN MS. COLMAN'S CLASS

A new series by Ann M. Martin

Don't miss #5
THE SNOW WAR

Ian trotted across the playground. A snowball whizzed by his head. "Hey!" he yelled. He turned around.

Ian saw Leslie packing a snowball. She ran into her fort and flung it out at the boys' fort. The snowball smashed against the side. It made a dent in it.

Now it was Bobby's turn to yell. "Hey! Hey, Leslie! It took me a long time to build that!" Bobby packed up a snowball. He flung it at Leslie's fort. It missed and hit the other one.

"Thanks a lot, Leslie!" shouted Karen. "That was *your* fault." Karen threw a snowball at Leslie.

The fight was on.

"Oh, boy," said Ian. He hurried to his rock. He tried to forget about the snowballs.